Stinky Steve Three

Ask Stinky Steve

Letters from Minecraft Fans

D1490479

Dear Stinky Steve,

My pickaxe always breaks at the worst times and I end up having to punch my way out of caves. My knuckles are still bruised from the last time. How can I avoid this?

Thanks,
Benny

Great question, Benny.

Well the first step is to make sure and mark your way with torches or wood blocks as you go, so you don't have to dig up to get back out.

I have a much easier time because I just follow the stinky brown cloud back to the entrance.

Dear Steve,

I've been building a castle in the desert for weeks and it gets sooooo hot. But if I try to work at night, I get shot at by skeletons and creepers keep blowing up my work. How can I keep cool in the blazing sun?

Dear Anonymous,

Wear a pumpkin on your head! Sometimes you'll inhale seeds, but you'll look stylish and keep from burning. My doctor warned me that it would put unnecessary strain on my neck, but then he passed out before giving me a better solution. I'm sure you'll be okay.

Here's an expert tip for you: You can't wear a pumpkin on your head if you are alreading wearing a helmet. Therefore you must drag the pumpkin into the helmet slot in your inventory.

Dear Steve,

I keep finding redstone circuits in caves that I didn't put there. Who or what might be doing this?

Thanks,
Wyatt

Dear Wyatt,

Sounds like you either have a hacker

or worse...Herobrine. The best thing to do

is just cut your losses and get out.

I recommend filling the caves with farts first before leaving. That'll teach whoever it is to mess with your stuff!

Dear Steve,

I've been working on a mine for about a week and I keep running out of torches. It feels like I have to bring a million with me every time. Is there a better way to light the place up?

Thanks,

SoFia22_HQ

Thanks for the letter, SoFia22_HQ,

My go-to method is to bring a flint and steel with me. Whenever it gets too dark, I just let one rip and use the flint and steel on it.

The smell lingers for quite a while, but the flame lights up a twenty block area. Just be careful that the air in your mine still remains breathable.

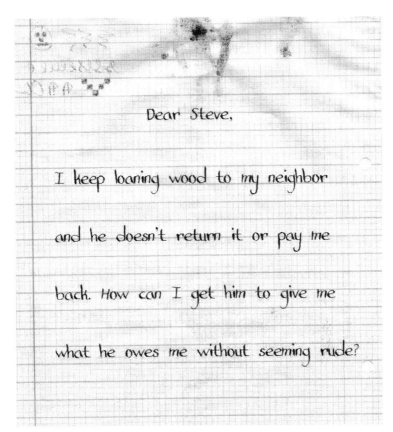

Dear Steve,

I keep loaning wood to my neighbor

and he doesn't return it or pay me

back. How can I get him to give me

what he owes me without seeming rude?

Dear Anonymous,

I've never had this problem because nobody wants to live near me (I'm not really sure why.) I'd recommend chopping your neighbors house down and claiming it was The Endermen.

Hi Steve!
Big Fan! I was wondering
if you have any tips
for navigating the end.
I can't seem to get
across the islands
without falling to my
death.
            ~Marta

Hmm. That's a tricky one, Marta.

I've had good luck with a fart propulsion

technique but that might not be an option

for you. Either install my bean mod and rip

away or throw some ender pearls across

to teleport you there.

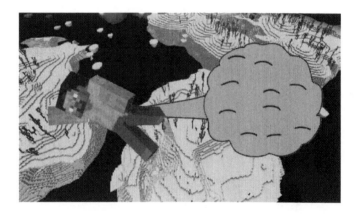

Dear Stinky Steve,

My brother likes baking cakes
but he keeps forgetting to
add the eggs. The cakes
always come out terrible and
neither of us want to eat
them. How can I help him
remember all the
ingredients next time?

Thanks,
The Baker Brothers

Dear Baker Brothers,

Have your brother sing a rhyme to help him remember the ingredients. I have one I sing before bed every night that goes like this:

"The moon comes up

and the sun goes down.

Don't sleep in your pants

cuz they'll turn brown."

Ah the memories! Wait, what was the question again?

Hey Steve,

I accidently
released the Wither in
the overworked and now
it's blowing everything up.
What do I do?!?!?!?!

Thanks!
Brittany

Don't worry, Brittany!

I know how to handle this! You're gonna need a big tower with a one-block wide hole that goes to the bottom. Stand inside and eat as much rotten flesh as you can stomach. Wait until the Wither is right over you, then point and shoot. With any luck, you'll break the sound barrier and punch straight through that nasty creature.

Look out below!

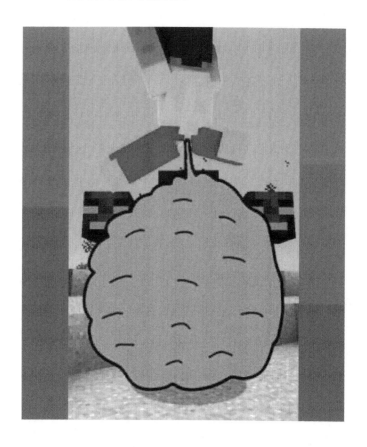

Dear Steve,

I live alone on an island. All my friends live on the mainland and have parties all the time. I'm so lonely, but I don't have enough materials to build a new house near them. What should I do?

~Trey

Dear Trey,

I know what it's like not to be invited to large gatherings. You should grow some trees on your island and harvest the wood. After a while you'll have enough to build a new house...or a giant statue of yourself. Which is way cooler anyways, and will make all of your friends jealous.

Who needs friends when you have

such a cool Minecraft statue?

DEAR STINKY STEVE,

I RECENTLY STARTED A
SHEEP FARM, BUT WOLVES
KEEP EATING THEM! HOW
CAN I KEEP THE SHEEP
SAFE WITHOUT LOCKING
THEM INDOORS?

SINCERELY,
JOSE

Dear Jose,

You should try taming the wolves. Offer them bones until they obey you. Then you'll have an entire dog army! While that might not be good for anything, I think it would be really cool. Don't you agree?

DEAR STEVE,

I BUILT A CHICKEN
COOP, BUT THEY
KEEP MANAGING TO
ESCAPE SOMEHOW!
WHAT SHOULD I DO?

THANKS,
GREG

Dear Greg,

It sounds like your chickens don't love you. Have you tried feeding them seeds and talking to them? Chicken's usually love hip hop. You can sing to them too.

If that doesn't work, make a fire moat around the coop with Netherrack and if they try to leave early, you'll be dining on cooked chicken that night. Yum!

Dear Steve,

I got myself into a bit of trouble. I was using TNT to mine and blew a big hole in the ceiling and lava started pouring out. Now I'm completely sur-rounded and have nothing to make a bridge with. Please seld HELP!!!!!!!

Dear Unlucky Minecrafter,

You'll probably be dead before you read this, but if you have a bucket of water you can pour it on the lava and turn it into obsidian. If not, it was nice knowing you!

And here's my impression of you: "AHHHHHHHH!"

DEAR STEVE,

I FOUND A JUNGLE,
BUT I DON'T SEE A
JUNGLE TEMPLE! I
REALLY WANT TO FIND
IT BUT THE LEAVES
ARE SO THICK IT'S
HARD. ANY TIPS?

Dear Anonymous,

My strategy in finding jungle temples, is to go deep into the foliage and let out a massive fart. As it spreads, it will kill all the leaves and make it easier to see in all directions.

But on the downside, anything lurking in that jungle will have a clear shot at you. It might be for you to bring some fish and bones so that you can train any ocelots and wolves that might be hiding. Good Luck!

Hey Steve,

A zombie pigman followed
me back through my
nether portal. He seems
really nice, but my mom
won't let me play with him.
What should I do?
Thanks,
MCZombiePig1

Can you believe it MCZombiePig1?

For some odd reason, parents are programed to look out for the safety of their young. Humans! Ugh! Just tell her you'll promise to ride a pig while you play with your new zombie friend. He wouldn't dare risk hurting one of his own kind.

Hello Mr. Stinky Steve,

My cat abandoned me to live in the jungle as king of the ocelots and now I can't scare off creepers. What should I do?

Your friend,
Craig

Dear Craig,

Forget the formalities, you can just call me Steve. Only my Mom calls me Stinky.

If you had treated your cat like royalty (as they expect you to), then none of this would have happened! My best suggestion is to get a dog and train it to meow.

Cats are real stinkers anyway.

Especially my farting feline named Stinky

Cat. Can you tell he takes after me?

HEY STEVE,

BRAD HERE! I'M GOING
MINECART RACING
WITH MY FRIEND TO-
MORROW AND SHE
ALWAYS WINS. WHAT
CAN I DO TO IMPROVE
MY GAME?

Dear Brad,

Here's what you need: Beans and a directional exhaust pipe. But if that doesn't work, try powered rails.

Hi Steve,
I love your books!
You are hilarious, I wish I
had fart powers like you.
So my question for
you is that I've
been trying to
raid an ocean
monument, but keep running
out of breath, what should
I do?

Thank you,
Sophia

Dear Sophia,

First off, thanks for the compliment!

Unfortunately the bean mod gave me

uncontrollable gas, but I've learned to put

it to good use by becoming Minecraft's

first superhero.

To answer your question, you can

enchant a helmet with the "respiration"

enchantment or make some potions of

water breathing.

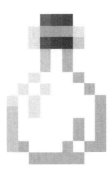

I've found both to work well. My

only problem is swimming through the

brown bubbles that trail me everywhere

when I'm raiding ocean monuments.

Have you ever seen a fart in the ocean?

It's not as pretty as you might think.

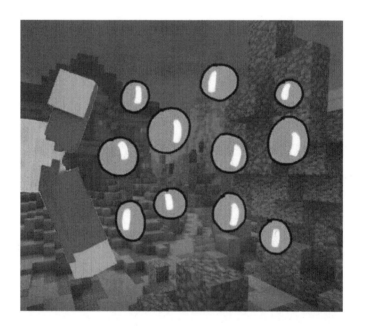

Dear Steve,

I think my friend is lost. He left
to go explore two days ago
and still isn't back. How can I
signal to him where our base
is?

Please respond!
`Brandon

FOR ADDRESS ONLY

48

Dear Brandon,

You can try building a tall tower and covering it with torches. If he doesn't respond to that signal, he's probably trying to avoid you. Did you fart in his lunch last week? That's happened to me many times.

If that's not the case, trying calling him. Maybe he's grounded from Minecraft for not eating his broccoli and now has to clean up all the dog poop in the backyard.

On second thought, if you call him, he'll just ask you to help him pick up the dog poop. It's probably best just to get a new friend.

Dear Steve,

I'll bet you think you're
sooooooo cool with your
smelly superpowers. But
guess what? Your days
are numbered. I'm coming
for you.

-The Burpinator

Ugg!! Not you, Burpinator!

That's not even a question. Go back to your own book! I'm outta here! *NEXT!*

Hi Steve!

I recently built a pool in my backyard and now cows and villagers show up uninvited! How can I keep them out?

Thanks,
Xavier

Dear Xavier,

You've got to trap a Zombie in a cage above the pool. That should scare off the villagers. But then you're still stuck with the cows.

Maybe you can throw a massive cow pool party and charge an entrance fee or open up a hamburger stand.

Burgers Anyone?

Dear Steve,

It's my brother's
birthday next week.
He loves Minecraft.
What should I get him?

Thanks a bunch,

-Jake

Dear Jake,

If your brother loves Minecraft so much, why doesn't he marry it? HA! HA! Pffft! Opps, I hate it when I laugh so hard, I fart. Excuse me!

For a present, how about a diamond sword or pickaxe? But if you're feeling generous, how about a portal to the Netherworld?

Steve,

what's your
favorite fart
joke?

Abby

Dear Abby,

Well to be honest, I've heard them all and while some are great, others just stink.

But try this one... Q: Why don't farts graduate from high school? A: Because they always end up getting expelled!

Good right?

Dear Stinky Steve,

For Halloween, I want to dress up like you, but fear my teacher will send me home for farting in class. What do you think?

Thank you,
Jackson T

Dear Jackson,

While I applaud your costume idea, I also don't want to get you in trouble. I remember my first day at school after I installed the bean mod; it wasn't pretty. I say save the Stinky Steve costume for trick-or-treating and dress up like a creeper during the day for two reasons:

First, when the teacher calls on you during class, you can avoid answering simply by hissing...Win!

Second, when you trick-or-treat at night as Stinky Steve, the people will give you extra candy just to get you to leave. But the downside is, your friends won't want to trick-or-treat with you.

The story of my life ☹

I built a really cool
tower but can't
jump off it and
sky dive because I
am in survival mode.
What's a fun way
to get down?

Derek

Dear Derek,

Just install my bean mod and your new found fart powers will let you fly all around Minecraft. Although, on the flip side, you won't be able to stop farting. So you may just want to switch to creative mode.

Dear Stinky Steve,

I had the most embarassing moment in school today when I bent down to pick up my backpack and I blew out the back of my pants and the kids all laughed at me. What's your most embarassing moment, Steve?

Thanks,
Notch

Dear Notch,

Wait, Notch? *THE NOTCH?*
Inventor of Minecraft? Well, I hope this is
you and not an evil trick by Herobrine.
But if it is you, it's an honor, Sir. Thank
you so much for writing in with a personal
question.

Every day in Minecraft used to be
embarrassing, but I can recall one-day in
particular when some kids told me it was

Bring Your Farts to School day and when I showed-up after eating Raisin Bran for breakfast, the whole class laughed at me for farting all over the room. I ended up walking home from school that day feeling so sad.

But you know what? It turns out the joke was on them. Ever since I turned my farts into a superpower, they aren't laughing anymore.

THE END...

...or is it?

Like the Book?

Be sure to leave a review on Amazon. The more reviews it gets, the more books I'll write. Don't forget to Tell a friend...

MEET MY FRIEND, PT EVANS, AUTHOR OF STINKY STEVE BOOKS ONE AND TWO!!

"It's Pooptastic!"

"Hey there, PT Evans is the name, writing books is my game. I love Minecraft, Pokemon, pizza, emojis, cats, and fart jokes (who doesn't?). When I'm not writing books or doing school visits, I can be found training alligators and sumo wrestling. Follow my adventures on Youtube, Instagram, Twitter, and Facebook." ~PT Evans

Twitter: @PTEvansAuthor
Instagram: @PTEvansAuthor
Facebook: facebook.com/PTEvansAuthor

MORE STINKY STEVE!!

DO YOU LIKE MINECRAFT? DO YOU THINK FARTS ARE FUNNY? See what happens in the wonderful world of Minecraft when Steve can't stop farting. Are the Creepers and zombies terrified – or attracted – to Steve's toxic smell? Can Steve find a way to overcome his flatulent issue, or will it get the best of him in the end? Find out in this fun new superhero series

More Minecraft books
by <u>PT Evans</u>

<u>App Mash-up: Minecraft and Angry Birds</u>

DO YOU LOVE MINECRAFT? DO YOU LOVE ANGRY BIRDS? What if you could play two Apps at once? Jackson and Susie love to play games on their Mom's phone. But today, a freak power surge sends them INTO their favorite games. What a treat – to be INSIDE an app - until they find themselves under attack by creepers and zombies and some very irate birds. A must read for Minecraft fans!

Minecat: A Feline Minecraft Adventure

Book One: A Whole Lot of Ocelots
Book Two: Sugar Cane Rush

DO YOU LOVE TO PLAY MINECRAFT? DOES YOUR CAT?? Spike is an indoor cat who spawns into his owner's game. It doesn't take long before Spike goes from ocelot bait to King of the Jungle. Will he decide to stay in the wonderful world of Minecraft? Can he stay clear of the zombies and creepers? What would YOUR cat do???

MONTAGE PUBLISHING

Connect with Montage Publishing
Twitter: @MontageBooks

Instagram: @MontagePublishing
FB: facebook.com/montagepublishing

www.MontagePublishing.com

42241462R00045

Made in the USA
Middletown, DE
08 April 2017